D0830114

SIHA TOOSKIN KNOWS

The Best Medicine

By Charlene Bearhead and Wilson Bearhead
Illustrated by Chloe Bluebird Mustooch

HIGHWATER
PRESS

 Canada Council   Conseil des arts
for the Arts   du Canada

We acknowledge the support of the Canada Council for the Arts.
Nous remercions le Conseil des arts du Canada de son soutien.

HighWater Press gratefully acknowledges the financial support of the Province of Manitoba through the Department of Sport, Culture and Heritage and the Manitoba Book Publishing Tax Credit, and the Government of Canada through the Canada Book Fund (CBF), for our publishing activities.

HighWater Press is an imprint of Portage & Main Press.
Printed and bound in Canada by Friesens
Design by Relish New Brand Experience
Cover Art by Chloe Bluebird Mustooch

Library and Archives Canada Cataloguing in Publication

Title: Siha Tooskin knows the best medicine / by Charlene Bearhead and Wilson Bearhead ; illustrated by Chloe Bluebird Mustooch.
Other titles: Best medicine
Names: Bearhead, Charlene, 1963- author. | Bearhead, Wilson, 1958- author. | Mustooch, Chloe Bluebird, 1991- illustrator.
Identifiers: Canadiana (print) 20190058692 | Canadiana (ebook) 20190058706 | ISBN 9781553798408 (softcover) | ISBN 9781553798422 (PDF) | ISBN 9781553798415 (iPad fixed layout)
Classification: LCC PS8603.E245 S47 2020 | DDC jC813/.6—dc23

23 22 21 20   1 2 3 4 5

www.highwaterpress.com
Winnipeg, Manitoba
Treaty 1 Territory and homeland of the Métis Nation

I dedicate Siha Tooskin Knows the Best Medicine *to the late Paul Crowe from whom Paul Wahasaypa gets his English name. An angel in the spirit world just as he was on earth, Paul smiles down on us all, as children learn about his grandmother's people through the stories in this series.*

—CHARLENE BEARHEAD

We dedicate the Siha Tooskin Knows series to the storytellers who taught us. To those who guided us and shared their knowledge so that we might pass along what we have learned from them to teach children. Their stories are a gentle way of guiding us all along the journey of life.

In that way we tell these stories for our children and grandchildren, and for all children. May they guide you in the way that we have been guided as these stories become part of your story.

—CHARLENE BEARHEAD AND WILSON BEARHEAD

Watch for this little plant!
It will grow as you read, and if you need a break,
it marks a good spot for a rest.

It was a cold and snowy winter day, but Paul Wahasaypa didn't even notice the weather. Paul didn't notice much of anything as he slipped in and out of sleep. He was in the hospital and not feeling well at all. Paul had started to feel sick a few days ago so his mom took him to the clinic. The doctor told Paul to stay home from school until he was feeling better. However, he didn't start to feel better. In fact, he just kept feeling weaker and weaker, so after a couple of days his mom and dad took him to the hospital.

The doctor was still doing some tests to see what was wrong with Paul. Ade had stayed all night with him while Ena went home to take care of Danny and Baby Laura. The whole family was very concerned about Paul. Ade had even taken a few days off work until the situation improved. He also had protocols in mind that he knew would help his son. Ade told Paul that he had to head home to do a few things and Ena would be coming over soon. He wanted Paul to try to eat some breakfast and rest a bit more while he was gone.

Soon after the food service staff had taken Paul's tray away the door to his room opened again. In walked Mugoshin and Ena, smiling at Paul. Paul tried to put on a brave front and look as though he was doing better so his mom and grandmother wouldn't worry. The truth was that Paul was as happy to see Ena and Mugoshin as they were to see him.

"Aba washdinno Mitowjin." Mugoshin greeted her grandson with a kiss on his cheek. Ena also

came over to give Paul a hug. She placed her hand on his forehead to check his temperature. "How are you feeling, Michish?" Ena asked. Paul just shrugged. He didn't feel much better but he kept hoping that would happen soon.

Mugoshin had set her bag down on the little table beside Paul's bed. She sat down in the chair beside the bed and took his hand in her hands. Mugoshin examined Paul's face thoroughly, looking to see what might be draining his energy. She stroked his hair gently for a while as she listened to his description of how he was feeling and what he was experiencing.

"Your mom called us yesterday, Siha Tooskin. She was very worried. She told us that the doctors are trying to help you, but your parents also know that our own healing ways are important. Your mom told us how much difficulty the doctors are having in trying to diagnose what is wrong, so she and your dad thought the doctors might need some help from us as well."

"Nitoshin is at home doing ceremony for you right now. He and your uncles will prepare the grandfather rocks and ask the Creator to help bring you back to good health. I know you are growing up and are on the path to becoming a strong young man, Siha Tooskin. Yet in some

ways, you are still a child, Mitowjin, and you need the healing medicine that comes from the grandmothers."

"I have boiled some medicine for you from the plants that I gather each summer and fall. I gather these plants to take care of my children

and grandchildren. I do this so that I can make this medicine even in the time of the snow when I cannot get to these plants. When you drink this remember that your belief and gratitude, along with the medicine itself, will help your body to heal itself. Before there were settler doctors like the ones you see in the clinic and hospitals today, the pediatricians were the women: the mothers, grandmothers, and aunties in our communities. Your dad stayed with the little ones this morning so your mom and I could come here to give you medicine. He is doing his part at home as well.

He will smudge your room and call upon the Creator to help you in the ways that are given to the men to do."

Mugoshin pulled a jar of liquid out of her bag. The mixture looked like tea, but Paul recognized it as the same kind of medicine that Mugoshin had given to his little brother when he was very sick as a baby. Paul looked knowingly at Mugoshin and she knew what he was thinking.

"Yes, you actually helped me to pick some of the medicines that I boiled to make this for you, Mitowjin."

Paul reflected on the time that he had spent with Mitoshin and Mugoshin late in the summer near the end of his school holiday. He remembered it well. That had been the first year that they felt Paul was ready to start learning which plants helped with particular illnesses.

Paul had understood at that time, just as he did now when it was he himself who needed help from the plants, that passing on the knowledge of the plants and their healing properties was a serious matter.

Mugoshin and Mitoshin had taught him that the plants also have a spirit, and they are to be treated with great respect, as they are giving up their lives on Ena Makoochay to help us to live in a good and healthy way. Paul recalled the words from his parents as he had prepared for the visit to his grandparents: "We don't take the medicines for granted or disrespect them, or they may not help us when we need them the most." Paul was so glad that he had paid attention and remembered to be humble and respectful the whole time that he was gathering medicine with his grandparents. He had only been given the earliest understanding in the summer and Paul knew there was much more for him to learn in the years to come, so he was grateful for Mugoshin's words to him now.

"You remember that with each plant we pick we offer words of thanks to Ade Waka and Ena Makoochay for providing us with the medicines that we need to keep us well. You remember that we offer tobacco to thank the plant families for sharing their gifts and giving their lives to help us. This is why

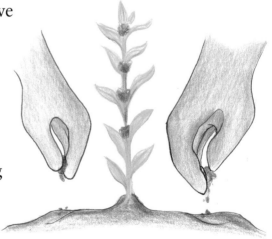

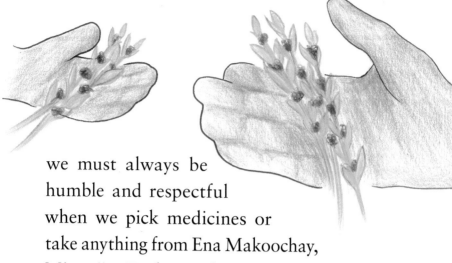

we must always be
humble and respectful
when we pick medicines or
take anything from Ena Makoochay,
Mitowjin. We know that there may come a time
when we need to use these medicines to care for
our children and grandchildren, our most precious
gifts from the Creator."

As Ena opened the jar and poured half of the
liquid into a small cup that they had brought from
home, Mugoshin reminded Paul, "The medicine
can't do all of the work on its own—we need to do
our part as well. It is our belief in the medicines,
our belief in the Creator, and our belief in our
ways that bring life to the medicines as well. We
would not take our children to a doctor we do not
believe in, nor would we use our own medicines

from Ena Makoochay if we did not believe in them and know they are good for us."

Ena passed Paul the cup. "As you drink your medicine, Michish, remember the words that you offered at the time when you helped to gather the medicines and gave thanks for all of the gifts in your life. Think about the beauty all around us—about the love of your family and all that Waka provides for us. As Mugoshin and I pray for you, you will pray for yourself—for good health to return to you."

Mugoshin walked to the other side of the bed and placed her hand on the top of her grandson's head. "You have so much love from your family, Mitowjin. Nitoshin is at our home doing ceremony with your uncles right now. Ade is taking care of your home and asking the Creator to help you. The love of your family, the strength of the medicine, and our prayers will all help you back to good health."

Paul thought hard about all of these good things in his life and his family. He offered his gratitude and in his mind asked the Creator for healing while he drank the medicine. He could feel the love and the strength of family as his mom, Mugoshin, and his relations asked the medicine, the grandfathers, and Waka to help him get better.

By the time Paul had finished the cup of medicine, Ena and Mugoshin had also finished with their prayers. Ena filled up Paul's cup with the rest of the medicine from the jar. "You need to finish this all up now, Michish. It will bring back your energy and strength."

"I will bring you a jar each day for three more days after this, Mitowjin," Mugoshin explained to her grandson. "You will drink one jar each day until all of the medicine that I've prepared for you is gone. The words that we have shared from our hearts and the properties and powers of the plants will work together. Soon you will start to feel better."

"Why do I have to stay in the hospital and take the doctor's medicine if you can just give me medicine at home, Mugoshin?" Paul sounded frustrated. He was already tired of being in this place.

"Remember what your dad taught you, Mitowjin," Mugoshin reminded her grandson. "Many of the medicines that are used by doctors in hospitals also come from the plants on the land. The white willow bark takes away the pain just like some of the pills that we buy at the pharmacy— the ones that help with a headache. The muskrat root that we use for a sore throat works at times like the cough drop we take from the store to find relief. We want what is best for our children and grandchildren. We need to embrace the best of all ways of healing for you."

Just then the door to Paul's hospital room opened again. A nurse came in to check Paul's

blood pressure and temperature. She gave Paul a little paper cup with two pills in it and a glass of water. "Here you go, Paul," she said with a reassuring nod. "You need to take these for a few more days. The doctor has most of your tests back and he thinks this will start to make you feel better soon."

Paul looked at his mother and grandmother with a little grin. He was already starting to feel better. Paul wasn't sure what each medicine was doing for his body, but he knew for certain that the best medicine for him was the love of his family.

Glossary

Ade	Dad or father
Ade Waka	Spirit Father or Creator
Aba washdinno	Good day
Ena	Mom or mother
Ena Makoochay	Mother Earth
Michish	My son
Mitoshin	My grandfather
Mitowjin	My grandchild
Mugoshin	My grandmother
Nitoshin	Your grandfather
Nigoshin	Your grandmother
Siha Tooskin	Little Foot (siha is foot; tooskin is little)
Waka	Spirit or Creator
Wayasaypa	Bear head

A note on use of the Nakota language in this book series from Wilson Bearhead:

The Nakota dialect used in this series is the Nakota language as taught to Wilson by his grandmother, Annie Bearhead, and used in Wabamun Lake First Nation. Wilson and Charlene have chosen to spell the Nakota words in this series phonetically as Nakota was never a written language. Any form of written Nakota language that currently exists has been developed in conjunction with linguists who use a Eurocentric construct.

ABOUT THE AUTHORS

Charlene Bearhead is an educator and Indigenous education advocate. She was the first Education Lead for the National Centre for Truth and Reconciliation and the Education Coordinator for the National Inquiry into Missing and Murdered Indigenous Women and Girls. Charlene was recently honoured with the Alumni Award from the University of Alberta and currently serves as the Director of Reconciliation for *Canadian Geographic*. She is a mother and a grandmother who began writing stories to teach her own children as she raised them. Charlene lives near Edmonton, Alberta with her husband Wilson.

Wilson Bearhead, a Nakota Elder and Wabamun Lake First Nation community member in central Alberta (Treaty 6 territory), is the recent recipient of the Canadian Teachers' Federation Indigenous Elder Award. Currently, he is the Elder for Elk Island Public Schools. Wilson's grandmother Annie was a powerful, positive influence in his young life, teaching him all of the lessons that gave him the strength, knowledge, and skills to overcome difficult times and embrace the gifts of life.

ABOUT THE ILLUSTRATOR

Chloe Bluebird Mustooch is from the Alexis Nakoda Sioux Nation of central Alberta, and is a recent graduate of the Emily Carr University of Art + Design. She is a seamstress, beadworker, illustrator, painter, and sculptor. She was raised on the reservation, and was immersed in hunting, gathering, and traditional rituals, and she has also lived in Santa Fe, New Mexico, an area rich in art and urbanity.